The Princess & the Pea

Story by:
Hans Christian Andersen

Adapted by:
Margaret Ann Hughes, Bill Angelos

Illustrated by:

Russell Hicks	Lorann Downer
Theresa Mazurek	Rivka
Douglas McCarthy	Matthew Bates
Allyn Conley-Gorniak	Fay Whitemountain
Julie Ann Armstrong	Suzanne Lewis

This Book Belongs To:

Amy Fletcher

Use this symbol to match book and cassette.

nce upon a time, in a castle that sat alone on a high mountaintop, there lived a king, a queen, and a prince named Dudley. Because the castle was so hard to reach, the family never had any visitors, so Dudley was lonely...very lonely.

The queen decided that Dudley should find a wife. That certainly would cure his loneliness. But the queen didn't want her son to marry just anybody...she had to be a real princess.

So Dudley set out to find a real princess for a wife. He traveled the world and met princesses of every shape and size. But although they were real princesses, there was something missing. Dudley returned home, sad and discouraged that he could not find a bride.

One night, the sky filled with clouds and rain poured onto the castle on the mountain. The lightning cracked and the thunder roared. Inside the castle, the king, the queen and Dudley sat by the fire drinking tea...when there came a knock at the door.

Dudley went to the big wooden door and slowly
opened it. There, standing in the pouring rain,
was a girl, and she was soaking wet.

Dudley asked the girl her name, but before she
could answer, she fainted.

Dudley carried the girl to the fire and wrapped her carefully in blankets to warm her. Lightning flashed and thunder boomed outside. Suddenly, the girl opened her eyes.

Both the queen and Dudley had so many questions to ask the girl, but the king wisely decided that she was too tired to answer them that night. He ordered a servant to take the girl to the guest room and give her dry clothes to wear. Dudley went to sleep wondering what the next day would bring. He knew one thing for certain…he could hardly wait to see the girl again.

The next morning was sunny and beautiful.

Dudley was happy to see that the girl was feeling much better. And when he asked her name, she said it was Katherine.

Dudley and Katherine walked and talked together in the garden all day. Katherine described every-thing they saw in such a beautiful way. A bird was a fairy messenger, a mountain was an enchanted giant. She made Dudley see things differently... and he liked it.

The king and queen, but mostly the queen, became quite worried that Dudley might be falling in love with the wrong girl. To show Dudley that he could be making a mistake, they decided to give Katherine the sensitivity test. Only a real princess could pass such a test.

The sun was beginning to set, and they didn't have much time. The queen rushed off to prepare for the test. She immediately ordered that every mattress in the castle be brought to her at once.

Servants dashed about every which-way and gathered up all the mattresses they could find.

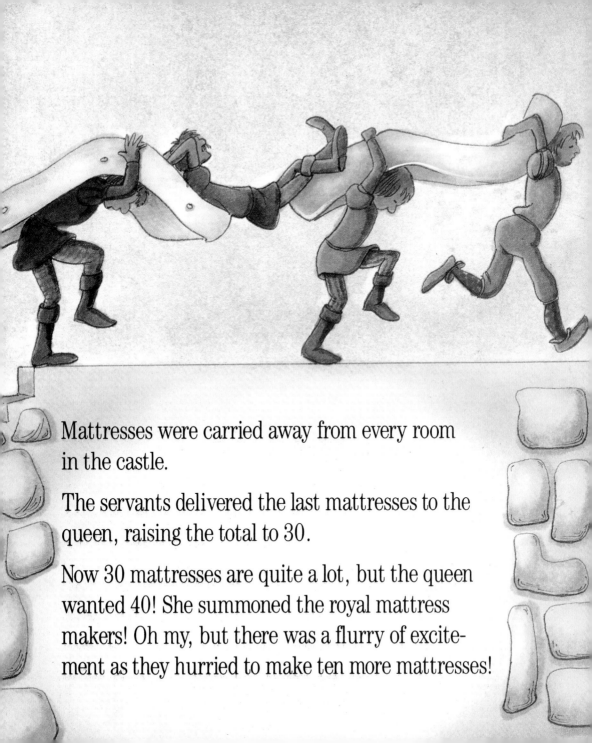

Mattresses were carried away from every room in the castle.

The servants delivered the last mattresses to the queen, raising the total to 30.

Now 30 mattresses are quite a lot, but the queen wanted 40! She summoned the royal mattress makers! Oh my, but there was a flurry of excitement as they hurried to make ten more mattresses!

They first made the casings for the mattresses, then they filled them with duck feathers, chicken feathers and goose feathers…Gasp!… GOOSE FEATHERS??!!

Feathers flew here and there and everywhere, as the royal mattress makers quickly stuffed the feathers into the casings…until… all 40 mattresses were ready.

The servants carried the mattresses, one by one, to the guest room, and there they stacked them up one on top of the other– higher and higher and higher still! The 40 mattresses rose 30 feet in the air!

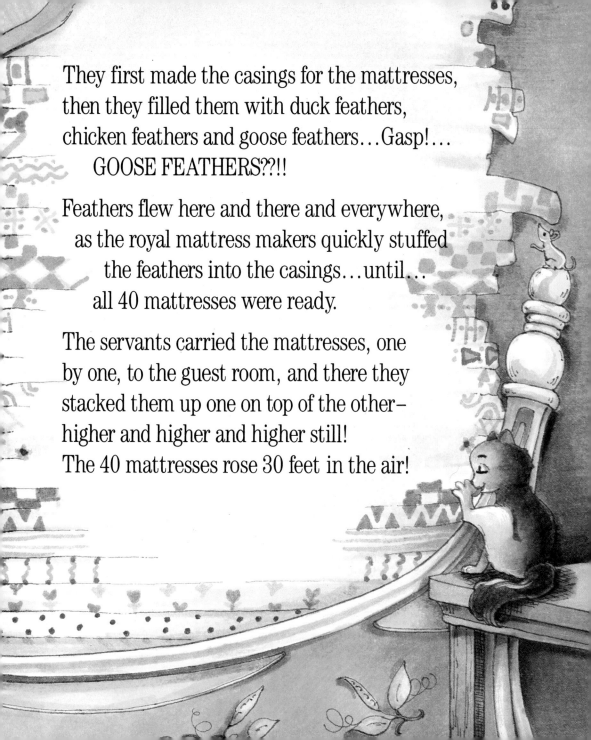

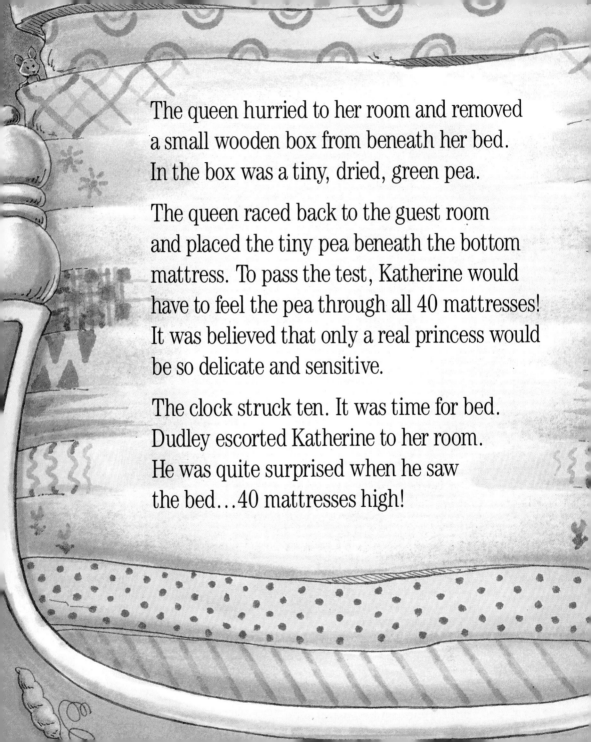

The queen hurried to her room and removed
a small wooden box from beneath her bed.
In the box was a tiny, dried, green pea.

The queen raced back to the guest room
and placed the tiny pea beneath the bottom
mattress. To pass the test, Katherine would
have to feel the pea through all 40 mattresses!
It was believed that only a real princess would
be so delicate and sensitive.

The clock struck ten. It was time for bed.
Dudley escorted Katherine to her room.
He was quite surprised when he saw
the bed...40 mattresses high!

A servant brought a very tall ladder, and Katherine climbed to the very top. Then she crawled into bed.

Dudley said "good night" to Katherine, then he and the queen left the room. In the hall, the queen told Dudley about the sensitivity test.

Dudley didn't care about a test, or whether or not she was a real princess. He sat outside Katherine's door on the cold, hard floor all night long, knowing in his heart that she was as good as any princess.

As much as Dudley wanted to help Katherine pass the test, he knew that he must not interfere. And so he waited, hoping against hope, that Katherine would feel the pea.

The rooster crowed as the sun appeared the next morning. Dudley went to the king and queen and spoke of his love for Katherine again. Then he asked their permission to marry her.

The king then told the queen that years ago, when he chose her for his wife, it wasn't the test with the pea but love that counted.

Well, after that, it didn't take long
for Dudley to convince the king and
queen that it didn't matter if
Katherine was a real princess or not.
Yet, when Katherine came down the
stairs, she yawned several times.

Something underneath the mattresses
had kept Katherine awake all night.
Whatever it was, it was so
small that when she tried
to find it, she couldn't.
You see, Katherine had
felt the pea!

Now even though Katherine passed the sensitivity test, everyone learned that sensitivity isn't something that can be measured. Sensitivity is much more than that. It is something that comes from deep inside…from the heart. Dudley and Katherine were soon married, and they moved to their own castle high on a mountaintop and very hard to reach. But it didn't matter, because Dudley was never lonely again.

nd they all lived happily ever after.